About the Author

I live in a small seaside town in Yorkshire. I have always loved books and enjoyed reading stories to my two children and my pupils when I was a teacher. I work in a windmill and rural museum and enjoy watching all the wildlife in the beautiful surroundings of the mill.

Millie's Windmill Adventure

Penni Tanton

Millie's Windmill Adventure

Nightingale Books

NIGHTINGALE PAPERBACK

© Copyright 2020
Penni Tanton

A CIP catalogue record for this title is
available from the British Library.
ISBN 978 1 83875 031 2

*Nightingale Books is an imprint of
Pegasus Elliot MacKenzie Publishers Ltd.
www.pegasuspublishers.com*

First Published in 2020

**Nightingale Books
Sheraton House Castle Park
Cambridge England**

Printed & Bound in Great Britain

Dedication

For James and Alexandra

It was a sunny, warm day in September. Mother Mouse asked Millie to finish her breakfast straight away and get ready, as they were going to go on an adventure. Millie got ready really quickly. She loved adventures!

They left their warm, safe home and carefully crossed the road towards the fields where Millie loved to meet her friends and play. Millie scurried happily along beside her mother.

"But where are we going?" she asked.

"Wait and see!"

They ran across a field full of swishing golden corn. Millie was itching to go and run and play, hanging from the ears of corn and swinging from stalk to stalk, just like she usually did, playing in the fields. But she still wanted to see where Mother Mouse was taking her.

All of a sudden, a dark shadow loomed over them.

"Oh, Mother! What is it? It is so big. I'm frightened!"

"Don't be," said Mother, "It is a windmill. We are going to see our friends."

Staying close to Mother, Millie crawled in through the small entrance.

"This windmill is where they make corn into flour. Come and see. You will like it. It is fun."

Inside they ran across some wooden floors, until they came to a round room at the base of the windmill tower. In the room they met Tom, the miller. Millie and Mother chatted to the miller, but soon Millie got bored and wanted to see more.

"Right, come this way," said Tom. "Follow me, but be careful! Do not touch the machines as they are big and heavy, but they do a very special job."

"What does it do?" asked Millie.

"Wait and see!" cried Mother and Tom smiling.

They all went upstairs in the mill. There were lots of steps to climb and they got higher and higher up the windmill tower. Soon they stopped on the bin floor. Here they saw grain being poured into a big pot, which Tom said was called a bin.

They watched as the grain whooshed down a chute, which made Millie laugh.

"Why is it in there? What is going to happen to the corn?" asked Millie, her bright eyes shining.

"Wait and see!" cried Mother and Tom.

They climbed down the stairs to the floor below. Millie watched the grain go down the chute and into a big wheel. But this wheel was made of stone. The grain poured into the middle of the stone.

Tom told Millie that there were two stones on top of each other and that the grain was being pushed into the centre of the stones. The stones were turning and, as they turned, they changed the grain into something else by crushing it.

"Is it magic?" asked Millie.

"No, but it is very clever. I will show you how the stones turn in a minute. But first let's find out what has happened to the corn."

"Oh, but how...?"

"Wait and see!" cried Tom and Mother.

They went downstairs to the floor below to see the crushed grain falling down a chute. Here it was collected into sacks.

"Oh, how clever! It looks like flour!" cried Millie

"It is flour." said Tom

"But what happens next?"

"Wait and see!" cried Mother and Tom.

They watched the flour being taken to be put into small bags. Mother said she would buy some later so they could make some bread.

"But you said you would tell me how the stones turn to make the flour." said Millie.

"Wait and see!" said Mother.

First, they had to go all the way outside. Millie was feeling quite tired as they had climbed up and down a lot of stairs.

Outside, the windmill looked very tall and had big arms.

Tom told her not to be afraid as the windmill did not have arms. They were big sails, and they couldn't reach to the ground. Tom said that when the mill was working, the sails went around in the wind, and inside there were wheels and cogs fastened to a pole. As the sails turned, the pole turned, and the pole made the wheels and cogs inside turn, which then made the grinding stones turn.

"Can I see the big wheels and cogs? Oh, I know... wait and see!"

They went inside, climbed more stairs and saw the big wheels and cogs turning. They heard the noise of the sails and the millstones grinding, and Millie smiled.

"It is like magic," she said.

"It is time to go home, and try making some bread, little one" said Mother gently. "You must be very tired."

"I am, but I love the windmill. It works hard to make all the flour," yawned Millie as they slowly set off to walk home across the fields.

"Mother, how do you make bread?" asked Millie.

"Wait and see!" said Mother.